Quiet Wyatt
Lexile: 400L
AR/BL: 1.5
AR Points: 0.5

Show and Tell Sam
Lexile: 240L
AR/BL: 1.6
AR Points: 0.5

Field Day
exile:
R/BL: BR
R Points:

Willie's Word World
Lexile: 410L
AR/BL:
AR Points:

Show-and-Tell Sam

and Other School Stories

Children's Press®
An Imprint of Scholastic Inc.
New York • Toronto • London • Auckland • Sydney
Mexico City • New Delhi • Hong Kong
Danbury, Connecticut

Dear Rookie Reader,

Do you like to **run and jump**?
Do you like **show-and-tell**?
Get ready to meet kids like you!
They each do something **special**
at **school**!

Have fun and keep reading!

P.S. Don't forget to check out the
fun activities on pages 124–127!

Contents

Field Day

By Melanie Davis Jones

Illustrated by Albert Molnar

Running fast.
Walking slow.

On your mark. Get set.

Go!

Mom and Dad
smiling proud.

Clapping hands.
Cheering crowd.

Egg and spoon.

Relay races.

Drinks and snacks.

Painted faces.

Hula hoop.

Balloon pop.

Toss the ball.

Time to stop!

Way to go.
Hip, hip, hooray!

What a great field day!

Show-and-Tell Sam

By Charnan Simon
Illustrated by Gary Bialke

Rosie's dog Sam
was going to school.

“You’ll be my show-and-tell,”
Rosie said.

SAM

Sam could hardly wait.

He showed Rosie
a shortcut to school,

and how to line up
at the door.

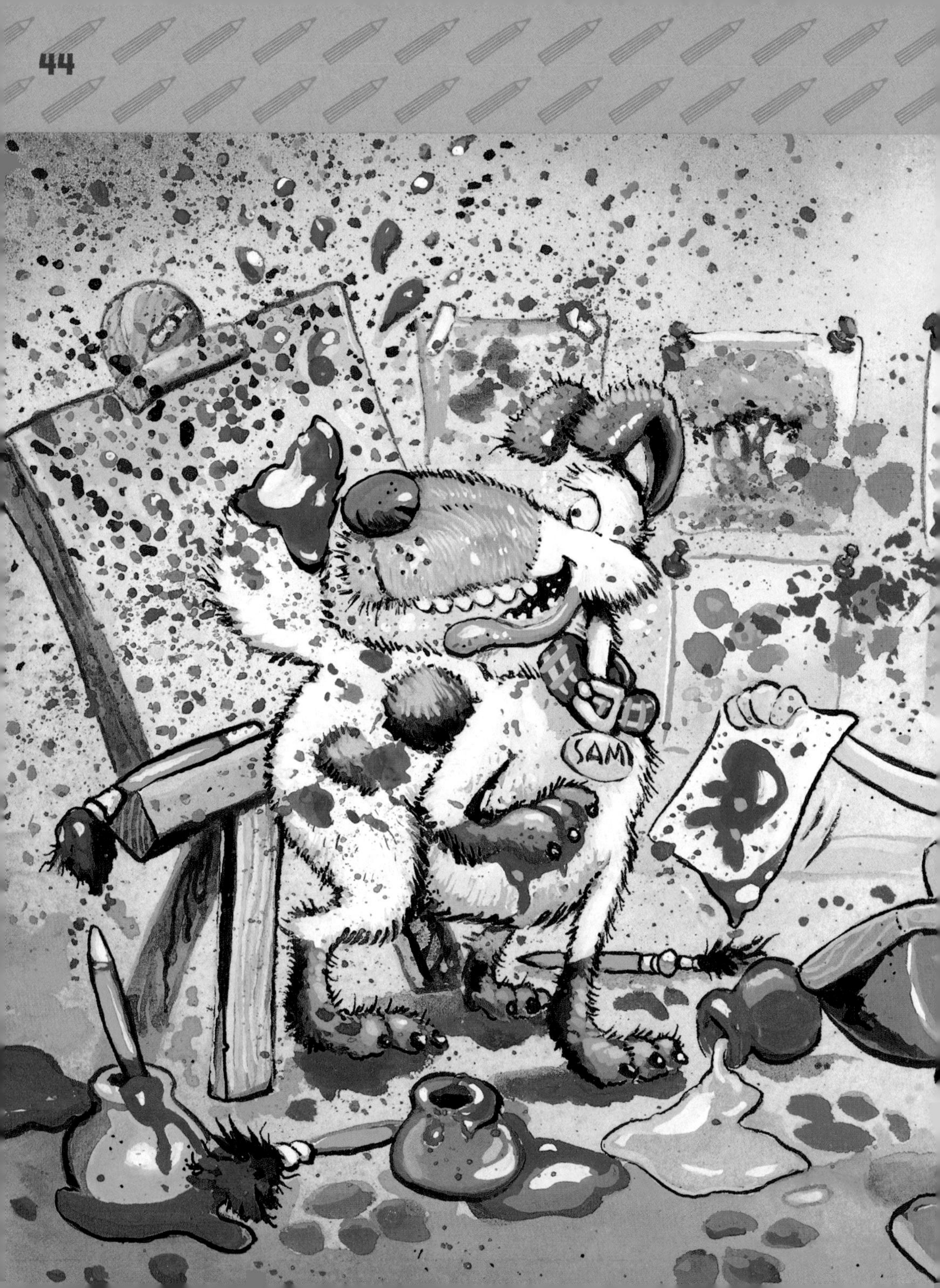
SAM

Sam showed Rosie's class
a new way to paint,

and sharpen pencils.

He showed them how
much he liked Teacher,

and tadpoles,

and singing,

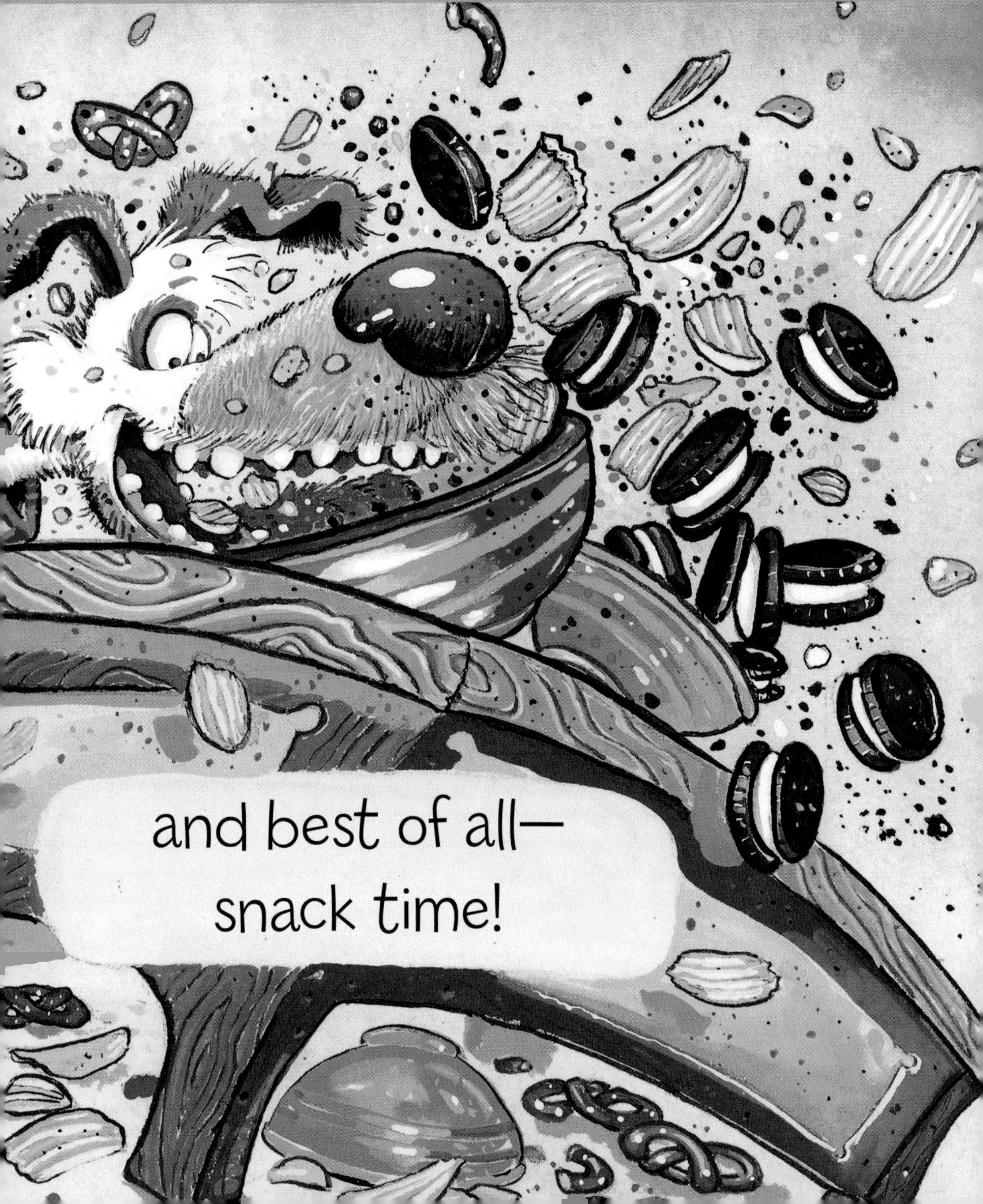

and best of all—
snack time!

Sam could tell the
class liked him, too.

Rosie could tell it was time to go home.

ACME
DOG
TRAINING
SCHOOL
2ND FLOOR
2ND FLOOR

Rosie's dog Sam
still goes to school.

ACME
DOG
TRAINING
SCHOOL

He misses snack time.

Quiet Wyatt

By Larry Dane Brimner
Illustrated by Rusty Fletcher

In a loud, loud town
is a loud, loud street.

On this loud, loud street
there is a loud, loud school.

And in this loud, loud school
stands quiet, quiet Wyatt.

Why is Wyatt so, so quiet?
Can he roar like a lion?

He can roar like a lion.
But today he's quiet like a mouse.

Can he howl under the moon?

He can howl under the moon.
But today he's as silent as the stars.

Can he rumble like thunder?

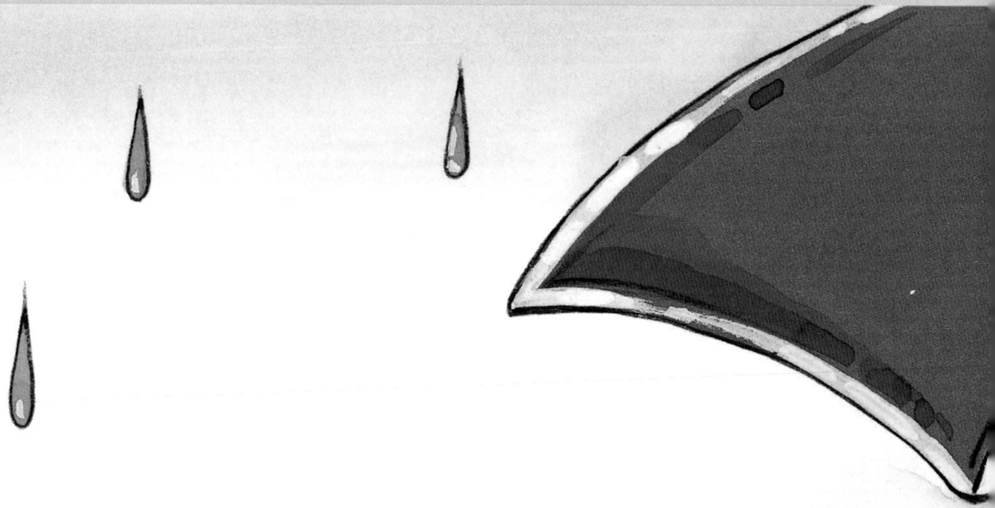

He can rumble like thunder.
But today he sounds as soft
as one tiny raindrop.

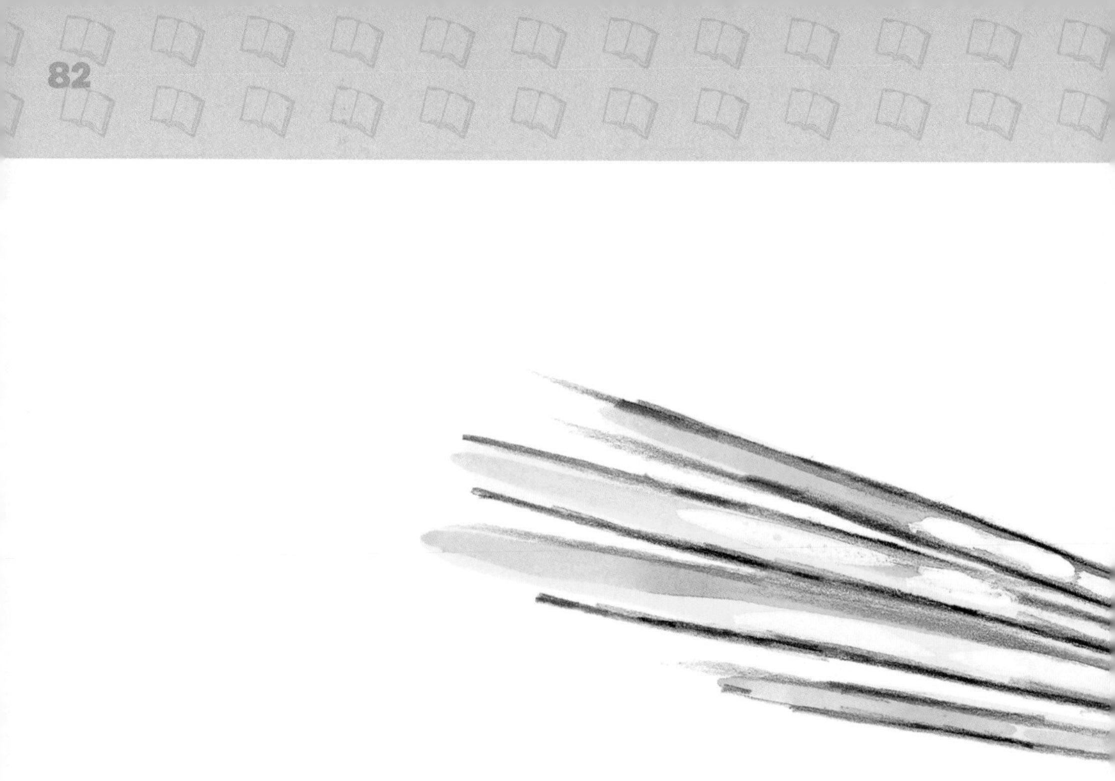

Listen to Wyatt roar like a lion!

Hear him howl under the moon.

Cover your ears when he rumbles like thunder!

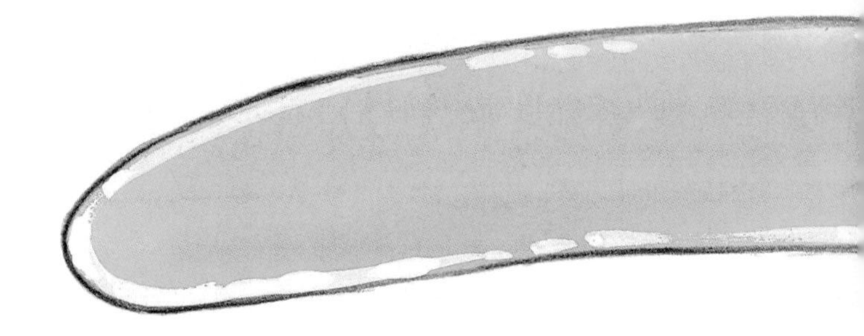

But not today.

Usually there's no one louder than Wyatt.

But sometimes it's good to be quiet!

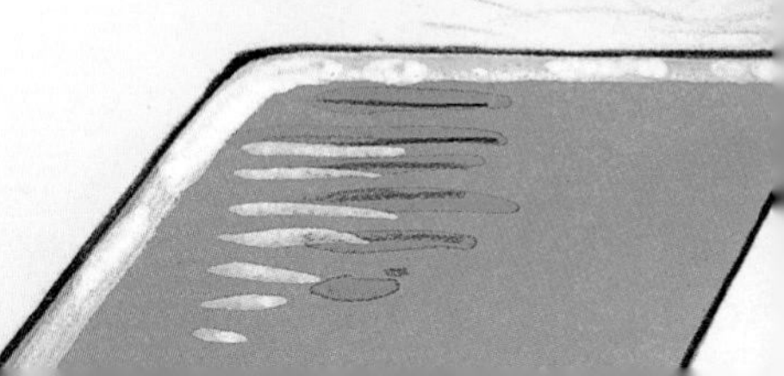

Willie's Word World

By Don L. Curry

Illustrated by Rick Stromoski

My name is
Willie. I love
words.

Today, Mrs. Walters wanted to play a word game. We had to make up silly sentences.

The words in the sentences
had to start with the
first letter of our names.

"Skinny swans swim secretly seaward," Sarah said.

What words start with W?

"Little Lucy licks a lizard lollipop," Lincoln said.

"Dizzy dolphins dive down deep,"
Danny said.

What words start with W?
Willie thought.

"Rats read recipes for rock soup," Ray said.

“Cockroaches can’t carry candy covered carrots,” Connor said.

What words start with W?

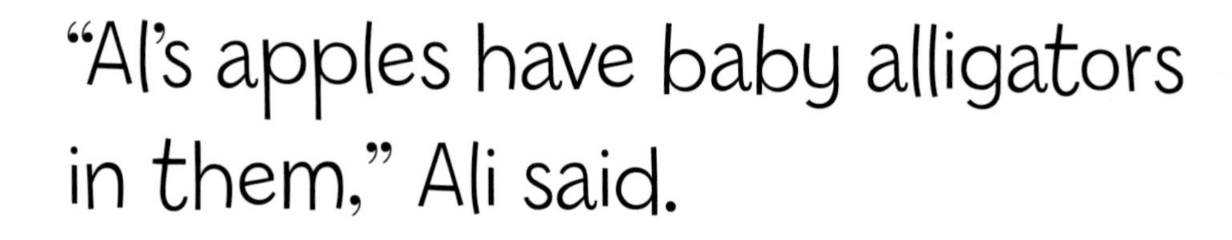

"Al's apples have baby alligators in them," Ali said.

“Pretty pigs eat peppermints with penguins,” Patricia said.

What words start with W?

"Ten toads tickle tiny tarantula toes," Tommy said.

"Big bubbles bounced like balls on the beach," said Brendan.

What words start with W?

"Chickens chased chunky chipmunks," Charlie said.

I need words with W!

"Walruses water-ski over
the waterfall in the winter!"
Willie yelled.

Wow!

Have a Field Day!

Match the words and pictures.

Hula hoop

Balloon pop

Ball toss

What looks like the most fun? Why?

Fill in the blank.

Sam ______ that he liked the teacher.

wrote **showed** **sang**

What else did Sam do at school?

Picture It!

Look at the picture.

What things are loud?
What things are quiet?

The Name Game

What's your name?
What letter does it start with?
Make up a sentence with words
that start with that letter.
Then draw a funny picture
to go with it.

Library of Congress Cataloging-in-Publication Data

Show-and-tell Sam and other school stories.
v. cm. — (A Rookie reader treasury)
Contents: Field day / by Melanie Davis Jones ; illustrated by Albert Molnar
Show-and-tell Sam / by Charnan Simon ; illustrated by Gary Bialke
Quiet Wyatt / by Larry Dane Brimner ; illustrated by Rusty Fletcher
Willie's word world / by Don L. Curry ; illustrated by Rick Stromoski.
ISBN-13: 978-0-531-21726-9
ISBN-10: 0-531-21726-4

1. Children's stories, American. [1. Short stories.]
I. Title. II. Series.

PZ5.S573 2008
[E]--dc22 2008008294

1 2 3 4 5 6 7 8 9 10 R 18 17 16 15 14 13 12 11 10 09